T0149359

LOVE'S DILEMMA

Carl Francis Forssell
also wrote

The Amazing Adventures of Big Nick in Alaska
and
Daring Alaska Rescues

LOVE'S DILEMMA

CARL FRANCIS FORSSELL

LOVE'S DILEMMA

Cover design: Dorina Boricean-Forssell
Back cover portrait: Dorina Boricean-Forssell
Text corrections Bruce Macdonald

This is a work of fiction. All of the characters, names, incidents, organizations, and dialogue in this novel are either the products of the author's imagination or are used fictitiously.

iUniverse books may be ordered through booksellers or by contacting:

iUniverse
1663 Liberty Drive
Bloomington, IN 47403
www.iuniverse.com
1-800-Authors (1-800-288-4677)

Because of the dynamic nature of the Internet, any web addresses or links contained in this book may have changed since publication and may no longer be valid. The views expressed in this work are solely those of the author and do not necessarily reflect the views of the publisher, and the publisher hereby disclaims any responsibility for them.

Any people depicted in stock imagery provided by Getty Images are models, and such images are being used for illustrative purposes only. Certain stock imagery © Getty Images.

ISBN: 978-1-5320-7946-7 (sc)
ISBN: 978-1-5320-7947-4 (e)

Print information available on the last page.

iUniverse rev. date: 07/30/2019

Contents

Kudos

A special thanks go to my wife Dorina who served as a tower of support during the innumerable hours I spent in writing *Love's Dilemma*. More notably, she offered suggestions for improving the story.

Carl Francis Forssell

1

Zipper Unzips

Skiers and snowboarders crisscross the steep slopes at the Alyeska ski resort (42 miles from Anchorage). Frank Carlton, 28, an expert skier, halts on an icy part of the slope. A female snowboarder screams and crashes into him. They are intertwined and slide twenty yards on the icy slope. They hit soft snow that stops their wild trajectory with the woman landing on top. They struggle up to a safe standing position. "Are you okay?" Julie Kittleson, 24, removes her ski helmet; her long blonde hair billows in the wind.

"The breath just knocked out of me," Frank bellows, and his eyes narrow.

"What the hell do you think you're doing; you could have sent us to the hospital."

"Oh, I'm so sorry, Julie stammers, I lost control when I hit the ice."

"From the way you crashed into me, I guess you haven't snowboarded for a long time." Frank's deep voice emphasizes a concern.

"You're right. This is my first time I snowboard. I'm a pretty good skier—I thought snowboarding would be easy."

"All snow sports are dangerous, especially for rank beginners. You could've killed me and you would end in the district court in Anchorage, be tried for homicide, and end up in jail. So don't be stupid, please take lessons before snowboarding alone again."

"I know I should have snowboarded much slower down the slope. I realize I don't know how to check my speed on a snowboard. Anyway, I just lost control and couldn't help it. I tried to make it to the toilet at the hotel at the end of the slope, and then I slammed into you. I'm so sorry. I feel so bad."

"Now calm down and stop talking so fast," Frank says.

"I'm so embarrassed."

"If that's all, you're very lucky."

"Can you forget this happened?" she asks.

"If you tell me your name, I'll forgive you for crashing into me." Frank smiles.

"I'm Julie Kittelson—she extends her shaky hand, I'm glad to meet you."

"Hi Julie, I'm Frank Carlton."

"Oh, oh. I need to hurry fast. I'm in pain—don't think I can hold it. Got go to the toilet real bad."

Frank points. "Let's head for that clump of trees over there." He attaches her snowboard to his back. "Stand on the back of my skis and hold me tight around my chest." Frank skis snail speed to the thicket. They stop at the trees and Julie disappears in the dark domain of the trees. She fumbles with a stuck zipper on her jump suit. She shouts, "Can you help me please?"

Frank tries to unzip the zipper, but the zipper remains stuck. "I can't unzip the zipper. If you agree, the only way is for me to rip open your jump suit."

"Gosh, I have to go to the toilet and fast. Please Frank rip open my jump suit."

Frank pulls down the jumpsuit over her knees thereby exposing her red underwear. *Wow, Frank thinks what a fabulous scene. Her well-developed breasts push against her red underwear.* In a hearty laugh, "Is this color the latest fashion trend for underwear?"

"No," she grimaces, "the latest fashion trend is getting me to the toilet quick."

He pulls his long parka over her. "Forget the trees. Let's ski down to the lodge where you safely can go to the toilet. Can you hold it?"

"Not sure, but we must hurry, I mean."

"Put your arms around me and we'll piggyback to the lodge. Make sure you stand firmly on the back part of my skis."

They arrive at the hotel.

Julie says, "I may turn into a smelly goat. I hope you don't have to hold your nose."

"Don't worry Julie. The last conversation I had with a goat about smell, he kept butting my butt."

Julie chuckles and says, "I'll meet you without a goat." She exits the rest room—she shakes her head, flaxen-colored hair cascades to shoulder length. Large, blue, expressive eyes, oval face, and small nose accentuate her beauty. "Frank, I'm so put out. Thank you for your help, and your parka. You saved my day."

"Take the parka home. I can get it later."

She glances at her watch. "I'm a flight attendant with Delta Airlines. I've got to go now to catch my flight to Tokyo. By the way, what is your work?"

"I'm a bush pilot in the search and rescue business.

"Tell you what, to get your parka come to dinner next Saturday night at seven."

"Here," Julie says. She hands Frank her business card with her home address.

"I'm already hungry. Can I bring my sourdough appetite?"

"I'll cook enough for a lumberjack."

"I want to know more about your search and rescue work. Until Saturday, bye-bye."

2

Could Be a Jerk

Julie and her sister Amanda, Ulland, 22, bought a duplex at Bunker Street, each of them has a self-contained apartment. Julie goes to Amanda's apartment to tell her sister about her adventures. "Today at snowboarding, I met a terrific guy. Holy cow, I crashed into him, we slid down the slope with him on top of me. Kinda wild."

"You mean you crashed into him and both of you were glued together."

"Yeah, sort of romantic, don't you think?" Julie smiles.

Amanda's eyes open wide. "Crashing in to someone isn't romantic. What's he like?"

"He's six feet, clean-shaven, looks like a young movie actor, His blue eyes twinkle, and his blond hair falls over his forehead. His name is Frank Carlton."

"How old is he?" Amanda asks.

"I'd guess he's about 28. He chewed me out, like a tough guy. Later his deep voice became calm. He has a great sense of humor;

his smile melts me. I've never met a guy before who turns me on so fast, Wow!"

"What's his line of work?" asks Amanda.

"He's a bush pilot in the search, and rescue business."

"Sounds like an exciting guy especially since he's a pilot. I like guys who fly. I've always wanted to meet one," Amanda says.

"I've never met a guy who bawls me out and then calms me down like this guy did. I had to go to the toilet really bad. When I broke the zipper on my jump-suit, he loaned me his parka."

"How romantic. Crazy! Be careful. Could be a jerk, calm you down more than you expect."

"He's interested, coming to dinner. What's going on with you and Gus?" Julie asks.

Amanda pauses, then says, "I'll tell you more after my date with him tonight."

3

Gimmi a Break

Gus Lochart, 27, leads Amanda into a ritzy restaurant in downtown Anchorage. The Maitre D' escorts them to a reserved table. Soft music sounds in the background.

Guests stare at Amanda whose black hair falls shoulder-length over her broad shoulders. Her large blue eyes are electrifying. Her pert, cupid mouth accentuates a perfect oval face. Her well-developed breasts peek out of her low-cut blouse. The guests also stare at Gus with his athletic body like a weight lifter. His clear-blue eyes contrast with his short-cut blond hair, his voice booms heavy and intense.

The wine steward presents a bottle. "We recommend Chardonnay. It's a dry white wine."

Gus nods, "I'll try it."

The steward fills Gus's glass with a small amount of wine. Gus tastes, sniffs, and shakes his head in approval. The steward pours two glasses.

Gus toasts Amanda. "Here's to our happiness. Here's to you

Amanda. By the way, my family has always celebrated with wine. Mom told me that she tried cooking with wine. She said it didn't do so well. After five glasses, she even forgot why she was in the kitchen."

"Ha-ha, that's a great one," Amanda raises her glass, pauses, and frowns, "I have something more serious to say that affects both of us. Gus your controlling ways bugs the hell out of me. You're not my supervisor. I'm not your employee. Your attitude is crappy."

Gus squints and raises his voice, "Well, Amanda your habit of always looking around at other men when you're with me insults me. I saw you look at that guy talking to that blonde when we sat at the table."

Amanda wrinkles her brow. Her eyes narrow. "That's bull. You have a weird imagination."

"I just saw you glance twice at that guy across the table."

"Gus, you're paranoid."

"What do you mean?" Gus bellows in a rage.

She whispers, "Gus! Please don't talk so loud. You know what I mean."

Gus says, "You shouldn't eyeball other men when you're with me."

"Are you still going on about that? You need help. You have to see a psychologist."

"Bull," Gus says, "stop staring at that tall guy again. We are getting out of here now. You're making a fool out of me." He jumps into his Jeep Grand Cherokee. Amanda follows him. He roars out of the parking lot to the narrow and curved highway. He drifts repeatedly over lanes.

"Hey Gus! Slow down," Amanda screams, "Oh, my god! You'll get us both killed."

"Don't tell me how to drive or to run my life," Gus retorts.

Amanda's voice falters, "You calm down and take me home now. I'm so stressed I feel sick."

Gus pulls up to the duplex where Amanda has her apartment

and hands her a huge box of chocolates. "Honey! I'm so sorry I lost it. Gimmi a break, forgive me. Let's not fight anymore."

Amanda rips open the candy box and shoves several chocolates in his mouth.

"I know it's all my fault," he mumbles. "I love you so much. I'll do anything to make you happy. Kiss me and forgive me."

"These chocolates are awesome," Amanda says. "I'd like to forgive you, but your overbearing character bugs me."

"Look Amanda, I'll buy you this kind of chocolates for the rest of your life."

Amanda continues to stuff her mouth with chocolates. Gus waits with patience to kiss her. Amanda, sick to her stomach, leaps out the car door, vomits, and rushes to her duplex. Gus runs after her, and she shouts, "Goodnight."

Gus feels remorse. "I'll call you tomorrow to see if you're okay."

* * *

The next day, Gus calls Amanda. "How are you feeling?"

"I'm okay," Amanda replies, "but we need to talk about our relationship and dating. You need temperament control therapy. If that works for you, we can resume our dating. Are you willing to do this?"

"It looks like I have little choice. I agree under these circumstances. I know I'll miss you so much."

Amanda frowns. "This may take time. I'll call a psychologist who specializes in Anger Management to see if he can help you to calm your anger dragon. I'll call you later."

After setting up the appointment, she calls Gus. "The doctor says that the therapy may take several weeks, depending on your progress. The doctor stresses there must not be any physical contact between you and me, but we can telephone."

Gus replies, "I'll miss you so much."

A week later, Gus goes to the doctor's office, enters and says to the receptionist, "I'm Gus Lochart, and I have an appointment at with Dr. Arnott."

The receptionist hands Gus a form.

"Mr. Lochart please fill in this form and give it to Dr. Arnott."

He takes the form and fills it in.

When he is finished with completing the form, he glances at a framed sign on the wall.

The Aims of Dr. Richard Arnott's Anger Management Counseling;
You will learn how to:
Best respond to fits of anger without being aggressive;
Identify times when your thoughts do not lead to logical or rational conclusions;
Relax, stay calm and be peaceful when anger erupts within you;
Apply problem-solving techniques to combat fits of anger.

The receptionist's buzzer rings. "You can see Dr. Arnott now"

Gus enters the office and hands the doctor the completed questionnaire. Dr. Arnott studies the answers to the questions. "Well M. Lockhart, I see from the answers to the questions that you suffer from intermittent explosive disorder."

Gus frowns. "Dr. Arnott, what is intermittent explosive disorder?"

"In the medical profession we call that IED for short. It is a common anger disorders. People with that disorder repeatedly have explosive, aggressive, violent behavior or angry outbursts. Research has revealed that about 16 million Americans suffer from IED. First of all, let us schedule ten sessions with me over a period of three months. You and I will see if we can cure you or reduce your IED."

* * *

A week later, Doctor Arnott proceeds with the first session and says, "We are finished with the first session. Do you understand what you have to do?"

"Yes, Doctor Arnott, I do."

"I'll see you every Tuesday and Friday at eight o'clock sharp."

Gus leaves the office and climbs into his Jeep. He muses, *I really don't know if I can stand waiting so long. It's this long waiting that contributes to my stress. What if Amanda chooses someone else? When I was young, I should've married Sally my high school sweetheart.*

4

A Line of Bull

Frank arrives at his apartment after completing a difficult rescue. He tosses his baggage on the floor, enters the bedroom, and shakes up his roommate Ray who is asleep.

Ray towers as skinny-as-a-rail guy with dark bushy hair, light brown eyes, and 28 years old. His extremely long fingers always fiddle something. When he less than frequently talks, his deep voice and diction is like a radio announcer's spiel. He graduated from the University of Alaska with an engineering degree. He works as a building inspector in Anchorage.

Ray grew up without a father, an alcoholic who disappeared after Ray's birth. Ray and his mother were on welfare and lived in a slum area. They were always hungry and underweight. In neighborhood street fights he usually lost and ended up with a bloody nose. When he was sixteen years old, he went to work at a local hospital when school was dismissed in the late afternoon. As an orderly, he worked in the emergency department where he checked in patients' clothes and valuables. There were times when he and a female worker had to transfer a body to the hospital morgue. There he saw decomposing bodies in different stages which, after a year, he delivered meat at night to various restaurants in downtown Seattle. As a student, school subjects were easy to master even though he spent little time on them. To finance his university tuition, he became a dog food salesman.

Frank nudges Ray again.

"Hey Ray I've got something fantastic to tell you."

Ray, yawns, and rubs his eyes. "What did you say?"

"Now hear this! A blond-haired beauty crashed into me on the ski slope. For once, a woman was on top of me instead of me on top of her. She's a beauty, reminds me of Grace Kelly, the movie star."

Ray nods, "I like on top introductions. I wish I could be so lucky. What turns you on with her?"

Frank replies, "Big, blue, eyes, blond shoulder-length blonde hair, a terrific body. It's love at first sight for me. What a babe! She's different. I know I'm a pushover with women. It's hard for me to explain. When I was younger, I was infatuated with two women at the same time. It's a weakness I've had for years. I just can't make up my mind. But now, I've never met a woman with such charm like Julie. Now, I'm going to concentrate only on one woman, Julie's her name."

Ray smiles and says, "You've told me the same story about Barbara, Joan, Laura, and others. You meet most of your women skiing or at the ski club. I like those same women, but they're always hot for you. You seem never to decide which one you want."

"Maybe to entice women to be hot for you, you should change your shave lotion—gain some weight so you aren't like a beanpole."

"Look! Wise guy. Every time I dance with a girl, you always cut in and sweet-talk her away from me."

"Is it my fault you don't know how to talk to a woman? When you talk about engineering problems with a woman, that doesn't turn her on. She probably will think about other things."

"Yeah, but I don't give them a line of bull like you do with your search and rescue work."

"If you can't play the game whose fault is it?" Frank asks.

"Look, I'm tired of your crap you've given me since we became roommates and friends five years ago. It's the same old story."

"Didn't your mother teach you anything about how to relate to girls?" Frank frowns.

Ray's eyes blaze, "Stop throwing me under the bulldozer or you'll be paying the rent alone. And, you'll have to get yourself a secretary to cover for you on the phone."

"Look, you're welcome to date any woman I'm involved with," Frank says.

"Okay Frank," Ray says, "I'll take you up on your offer. I'll be at the next dance."

Frank goes to the kitchen. While he cooks, he thinks, *hey, maybe I made a mistake. I better not be so generous to let Ray date Julie and Amanda. He might snitch the girl I want and I would be out in the cold with neither girl whom I would choose to be my happily married wife.*

5

Tango for Two

Three days later, Frank returns to his apartment from a rescue, throws his flight bag on a chair, sits on his bed, and lifts thirty-pound weights in each hand. The phone rings. He drops one of the weights, reaches the phone, and continues working the other arm.

"Hello, Carlton speaking."

Amanda sits at her desk at the library.

"Hi, Frank. This is Amanda. Julie had to fill in on the Seattle run at the last moment. She left at three this morning—she didn't want to wake you up. She wants to take a rain check for her date with you."

"Sure, I know that airline assistants schedules are sometime chaotic that requires them to cancel at the last moment important meetings and get-togethers."

"Thank you for understanding. She is so sorry. She'll return in three days."

"Hey," Frank says, "I have two tickets to a folk dance at the ski club this evening. How would you like to go?"

"Sounds like so much fun. I know Julie would urge me to go.

Julie wouldn't mind, but I'll call her now to confirm." Minutes later, Amanda calls Frank. "It's Okay with Julie. I'd love to dance." She gives Frank a card with her address and her phone number. "I live in the north-end duplex. It's marked with a bronze metal address tag 'Amanda Ulland, apartment A'. Just ring, I'll be there.

"Pick you up at seven."

Amanda hangs up the phone, smiles in anticipation, and slaps her thigh with a glint in her eye.

She mutters, "Just you wait Mr. Pilot."

* * *

Frank and Amanda enter the ski-club dance-floor. Frank leads Amanda to Ray's table and introduces Ray to Amanda.

"Ray, meet Amanda, Julie's sister. Julie couldn't make it."

"Nice to meet you, Amanda."

"Likewise." Her eyes sparkle as she shakes hands with Ray.

Frank guides Amanda to the dance floor to wait for demonstration tango instructions. He glances at an old girlfriend who appears to be drunk. Her partner holds her up from stumbling and falling to the dance-floor.

Amanda raises her brow, "I'm out of practice. Sometimes I feel like I have pebbles in my shoes. I don't worry about it anymore, but I'm always sorry for my partner."

"Don't worry about my toes. They are tough. Let both of us let it all hang out in the dance. Take the bun in your hair out."

She releases the bun, flips her hair.

"Your hair is so exotic. With your hair down, you look like a new Amanda."

"Let's burn up the floor," she says.

The small band plays a Fox Trot. Frank and Amanda dance as if they have danced the Fox Trot many times before. She oozes sensuality with her sultry voice. Frank holds her tight. "The smell of your perfume makes you a sexy girl." He holds Amanda close. The music stops.

The instructor knocks on a microphone with his finger.

"Your attention please! Tonight, my partner and I will show you the Tango. You should follow our movements as best you can. I'll give your lady partner a number. She should pin the number on your back." The instructor hands out numbers to the participants. Frank's number is five.

Frank asks Amanda, "Have you ever danced the Tango?"

"Well, I learned it in a dance class at high school. I haven't danced the Tango for a long time."

Frank nods, "let's try it."

Amanda frowns "I might screw it up."

"Don't worry, Amanda. Just follow the rhythm with me."

All dancers take the traditional tango ballroom stance. Frank leads Amanda through the preliminary steps. The instructor nods his approval.

Frank leads Amanda through the preliminary steps, and whispers in her ear, "You are doing fabulous. Now let's change steps and positions as the instructors showed us. When I swing you around, try your best steps." The band plays the *La Cumprasita*. Frank and Amanda with other couples tango around the ballroom counterclockwise. Frank leads Amanda and bends her near the dance floor. Amanda kicks up her leg and hooks Frank's leg. They trip and both sprawl on the dance floor.

"Wow, Amanda you sure know how to squeeze a man's leg."

"Oh, I'm so sorry that I threw us off balance."

"Why, landing on the floor with you is like landing a plane on the ground, a little bumpy. Just kick up your beautiful leg not so tight, and we won't trip."

"Okay Frank, I'll do my best in the future. That was a great lesson. I'd like to continue The Tango. It's so much fun and beautiful and so sexy. Living it up like this is what I need."

"The tango may be too sexy for you. Julie wouldn't like that."

"Are you kidding? You should've seen her do her wild dances in high school, like the Dirty Boogie. For a sister two years older than me, the guys thought she was much more sensuous."

"Was she your role model?"

"Not really. We've different personalities. She's more outgoing than I am. I'm reserved."

Frank's former girlfriend, Brenda, who also takes instruction, steps over to Frank and Amanda.

Brenda—intoxicated. "I see the kind of rescues you make when you tell me you'll be out of town. Your old socks smelled so bad I put I put them in the trash can. Good luck to your lady. She'll need it."

Frank turns to Amanda. "She gets that way when she's loaded. I feel sorry for her."

Amanda says, "She's not sorry for you."

"That's to be expected from a crazy woman."

At the end of the instruction, Frank and Amanda sit at a table. Frank orders wine, and says,

"You seem just as friendly as Julie."

"Frank, you see, Julie's the life of the party. But I guess at times I'm like a wallflower. Guys are much more attracted to her."

"I don't believe it when it comes to beauty. Perhaps you are reserved and Julie is outgoing. As beauty is concerned, your face is just as lovely as hers."

Amanda asks, "Are you a beauty expert? What are your qualifications? Let's not compare looks, it gives me an inferiority complex."

"No, I'm not a beauty expert, far from it. But my mother taught me something about beauty and even marriage."

"And, what was that?"

"Before marrying a beautiful woman, keep both eyes open. After marriage, keep one eye closed."

Amanda says, "After marrying a beautiful woman, you should keep both eyes closed."

"You're right. You know the old saw, marriage is not always made in heaven, and beauty is the gift of the gods. The two aphorisms don't always agree."

"That's right about beauty."

"For me," Amanda says, "there's beauty in the wild blue yonder and everywhere."

"Speaking of the wild blue yonder, how d'you like to go flying tomorrow?"

"Does your plane have parachutes?"

"Only one. You'll have to jump with me. As we float down, give me a bear hug. We can get to know each other better that way."

"That doesn't sound very romantic."

"Oh it is. As we float down, I'll kiss you at 6,000 feet altitude. That'll be romantic."

"Is that what you call falling in love?"

"It all depends on our landing. We could be in love or pain."

"And, if we land upside down?"

"Call it crazy love. Amanda, can I borrow a few dimes? It's an emergency. I'm supposed to call my mother when I fall in love."

"I'm out of dimes. But, I'll give you a few nickels if you take me flying. I'm off Tuesday from my work at the library."

"I'll fly you to the moon next Tuesday."

"But, don't fly by the seat of your pants."

"I'll wear long underwear." Frank says, "I'm feeling kind of dizzy due to the altitude right now. Can I have a hug?" He hugs Amanda.

Amanda says, "So soon? Only my hugs?"

"Was ten seconds too soon?"

"It depends how often you blink."

"I'd never close my eyes over you. When I pick you up at 7 A.M. Tuesday, my eyes will be wide open."

"I'll be waiting for your open eyes. Goodnight."

Frank in his apartment gathers up the beer cans and sweeps the floor. The phone rings.

"Carlton speaking," he says.

"Hey Honey," Julie says, "I just want to tell you how sorry I missed our date. I'm finally in Tokyo. Did Amanda call?"

"Sure did, she explained everything."

"Miss you."

Frank says, "That makes two of us."

"Got to go to board my flight. I'll be back soon. Bye-bye."

Frank worries, *I have to watch myself or I'll botch this whole romance before I can choose to get serious either with Julie or Amanda.*

6

Not Too Fast

Wow, thinks Frank, *when I talked on the phone with Julia in Tokyo, I felt like she really loves me. I must get some superb wine before Julie returns.*

He heads for a La Bodega on East Benson Boulevard to replenish his stock of wine.

* * *

When Frank is away, Ray finds Amanda's phone number from Frank's notes on the telephone table and calls Amanda.

"Hi, Amanda this is Ray, Frank's roommate."

"Hi, how are you?" Amanda replies.

"Still kicking. The airlines are having their annual ski races at Alyeska this Saturday and Sunday. Would you like to go?"

"Love to. I'm free on Saturday."

"I can pick you up at 8 A.M. How do I find you?"

"I'm in the duplex at 1765, apartment B Bunker Street, the

apartment on the north side. The bronze metal tag says Amanda Ulland. I'll be waiting."

* * *

At Alyeska, Ray and Amanda clap hands for the winner of the downhill race. As they walk toward the lodge filled with skiers, they hold hands.

In the lodge, Ray finds a table and orders wine. Later, the wine gets them in the mood to dance the Polka.

They assume the starting position, whirl, and tap their feed to the music. Ray says, "We dance so good it's like we've danced before."

"Maybe in our dreams," she says.

"Ray, thank you so much for inviting me. I have had little time to have fun. I need more of this."

"Consider me your fun man."

They raise their wine glasses.

"Here's a toast to our fun." Ray clinks Amanda's glass. "You know, Amanda, it would be fun to know you better. Tell me something about your life."

"Getting to know someone is like opening a safe. You have to learn the number combination before you can take anything out."

"What's your combination?"

"I'll start from the first number. I'm a librarian. And your life, Ray?"

"As a structural engineer, I need your card for a fast check-out for books."

"Any time, but not too fast. Ray, I've got to go. Thanks for the fun time."

When Amanda leaves, Ray thinks, *Wow, what a gal. She and I could certainly have a wonderful life together. We seem to have the same ideals. But I wouldn't want to lose my friendship with Frank who would believe I stole his choice of gals to marry. I better watch my step, or I could lose both Amanda and Frank.*

7

Tame the Tiger

On Sunday, Frank calls Amanda.

"Would you like to go flying today?" Frank asks.

"I'd love to. Sunday is my day off," Amanda replies.

"I'll pick you up at nine in the morning."

Frank flies them to his cabin on the Kenai.

At the cabin, Amanda is impressed at the workmanship and sits at a bay window. "I love the view. Your cabin is so rustic. Was it difficult to build?"

"Built it myself and installed a generator for electricity. Took me two years to build."

"Is there anything you can't do?"

"Well, entertain a woman like you."

"I'd say you're doing a great job."

Frank prepares brunch and serves Amanda at the table.

"Your breakfast is fabulous. The reindeer and cheese omelet together with the salmon are terrific. Who taught you how to cook?"

"As a bachelor, I had no choice. Do you like bananas or strawberries with pancakes for breakfast tomorrow morning?"

"I'll never make pancakes tomorrow."

Frank says, "I have little talent in the kitchen, but I can do light housekeeping."

She scrutinizes the room. "You need a housekeeper."

"Let's drink to that." Frank pours two glasses of wine and turns on the radio with dance music. "There's a new drink made with whisky and carrot juice. You get loaded and find your sight better in the morning."

Amanda says, "I'd mix it with tequila and you'll do the Mexican Hat Dance."

Frank pulls Amanda to her feet and they dance, his face flushes. She snuggles provocatively close to him.

"There's something about you that makes you special."

She whispers, "Maybe it's the booze."

Frank says, "Then I'd like to get drunk over you. Your kisses put me in a swoon."

Frank kisses Amanda passionately. She trips over the carpet and they land on a squeaking couch. Their passion intensifies.

"Why don't you fix your couch?"

Frank catches his breath, "At a time like this? Let's relax in a better place."

She turns her head and looks lovingly into his eyes. "Is that what they call it? I don't need a better place. I'm fully relaxed now."

"I didn't mean that. You know what I mean. We are turned on."

"Speak for yourself. Are you trying to seduce my mind so you can have my body?"

"I want your body and soul."

Amanda's eyes narrow, "You've got the wrong order. Try my soul first."

They rush into the bedroom and tumble onto the bed. Frank slips his hand to the top buttons of her blouse and unbuttons the first three.

"Whoa, Tiger—take it easy." She slaps his hand, rises up quickly, and walks to the door. Frank catches her. "I thought the feeling was mutual."

"Wrong! You didn't hear me. If you think I'm ready for love making at this stage, you've got the wrong babe."

"Your eyes have an icy stare."

"At this moment, yes. Look, big guy. I'm not a one-night stand. Find that at the Blue Moon Bar. That's where guys can hang out when there're in town. The babes are easy makes there, so I've heard."

"How do you know?"

"The last guy I was with stomped out of my apartment in anger when I wouldn't make it with him. I asked him where he was going. He said he was going to the Blue Moon Bar where the girls aren't old-maid prudish."

"I guess I knocked at the wrong door at the wrong time. It's just that I couldn't tame the tiger any longer."

"In the future, take better care of your tiger."

"I'll train the tiger better."

"That remains to be seen. I'm ready to go home."

"I understand your feelings. Sorry."

On returning to his apartment, Frank wonders, *I hope I don't get confused and lose both Julie and Amanda. I guess time will tell, but I have to watch myself so I don't repeat my past mistakes. Now I want to have only one love, and I'll have to be very strict with that, too. But which one will it be, Julie or Amanda. I'm nuts about both of them, but for different reasons. Maybe I should go to see a marriage counselor.*

8

Nixed Sex

Frank wakes up early the next morning with dreams of Amanda circulating in his mind. He picks up his cell phone and calls her. "Hello darling, I miss you very much."

"I'm terribly sorry. I had too much to drink. Will you forget last time?"

"I'll forget it for now."

"Could I see you again?"

"I will work-out for my mile swim tonight at my friend's private indoor pool. You can meet me there at seven this evening."

* * *

Frank meets Amanda at the pool and gasps as he looks at her breathtaking body. They dive into the pool. Amanda swims the Australian crawl on the start of her routine mile-swim. Frank keeps pace with her. At the end of her mile, Frank touches her arm, they exit the pool, and sit on the pool's edge.

Frank breathes rapidly and asks, "Do you know how to give Cardiopulmonary Resuscitation?"

"Why?"

"Because keeping up with you just collapsed my lungs."

"When will you get back to reality?" Amanda asks.

Frank says, "Let's get back to reality in the Jacuzzi. There's no one else here, we can have the Jacuzzi to ourselves."

They enter the Jacuzzi and sit next to a strong jet of water. Frank opens a bottle of wine. He pours two glasses of wine and hands one to Amanda. Both become super-relaxed with the help of *old-friend* wine.

"This is so relaxing—Oh-la-la I could go to sleep with no trouble," Amanda says.

"Are you tired?" Frank asks.

"Not really, but I'm in a state of bliss."

"You should be tired because you've been dashing through my mind since I saw you. I want to know more about you—have you ever been married?"

"Nada, I decided to be an old maid."

"I'm sure you've broken many hearts?"

"Well to tell the truth, my heart never told the truth."

"Maybe the men's hearts told the truth. I don't know how to say this, but you have truly stolen my heart."

"I haven't yet met a man who told me the truth about love and hearts."

"Would you believe my heart if I told you you're very special for me?" Frank asks.

"If you tell me it depends. But I'd have to know you better. It'll take some time."

Frank pulls Amanda close to his chest. They kiss passionately. He slips his hand to her bikini to untie the string. Amanda shoves his hand away.

"Not in the mood?" Frank asks. "Do you believe in love at first sight, or should I creep past you again?"

"Without the heart, I don't know what it is to love someone, but I do know what friendship is."

"With you, friendship will turn my heart on fire," Frank says.

"Let's start with friendship."

"Sure, friendship can develop into love when your heart is ready. Can you ever promise yourself that you'll try to love a man hoping he will always love you? Why that puzzled look?"

"How can I make that promise," Amanda asks, "like when all my summer romances were flops?"

"When that happens, you have to never give up—a guy out there waiting to give you his love."

"I wish he'd show up soon, I'm tired of waiting."

"That guy has arrived. Try me," Frank blurts out. "If you haven't tried again and loved, you haven't lived a life at all."

"From the romantic stories I've read, if you love someone, don't grab too tight. If they come back, it's real love. If they don't, forget it. And that has happened to me with men."

"If I love someone, love has a special connotation," Frank says, "Do you know that the Eskimos have 52 words for snow because it is so special to them? There ought to be as many for love."

"You seem to know the subject of love. Are you speaking of your experience?"

Frank admits, "My affairs have been losers most of the time. Loved and lost because I couldn't decide, or the girls couldn't make up their minds."

"In my case, men have left me cold. This is the first time Julie and I have been interested in the same man—you."

"That your interest in me makes me thrilled and honored. It is great to meet you again. I've got an early morning search, but I'll be looking forward to seeing you soon." He pulls Amanda to her feet, and plants a kiss before leaving.

I better watch my step, Frank worries, *otherwise Both Julie and Amanda will think I'm playing games with them.*

9

Hung Low

Julie returns from her flight exiting a cab with her carry-on luggage, enters her apartment. After unpacking, she goes to Amanda's apartment, knocks on the door, enters, and embraces Amanda. They sit at the kitchen table and drink coffee

Julie asks, "What do you think of Frank?"

"He seems like a nice guy. Since he had two tickets to the dance—you couldn't go—so I went with him."

"Thanks for filling in. Did Frank seem disappointed at my no show?"

"I think he wished you were with him."

"I never met a man who attracted me so fast. How did the dance go?"

"We had a great time. We practiced the Tango and other dances."

"How long did you stay?"

"He dropped me off at one in the morning."

"Did he try to kiss you?

"He just shook my hand and said goodbye."

Julie says, "He promised to take me to his cabin. I wonder why he never called."

"I'm sure he will. I think he's a man who keeps his word."

* * *

Frank and Ray lounge about their apartment. Soon, the discussion leads to Julie and Amanda. "Ray, I've got the hots for Julie. I thought I finally met just one woman really to love. Then I met Amanda. With Julie, it is love at first sight. Now it's the same with Amanda."

"Here we go again," Ray says, "so now you're in love with two women at the same time?"

"I can't help it. They both blow my mind. Both are knockouts, loveable, and so sexy."

"Well, I understand. I could even flip out over Amanda."

"Amanda has wild bedroom eyes, a sensual look. She intrigues me especially with a voice that sounds like a whisper," Frank says.

"You don't know much about these women. Right?" asks Ray.

"They both seem so affectionate in their temperament I can't help that I love them."

"They could be frigid, and you'd want to kick them out of bed," Ray says.

"But they seem so honest in their feelings."

"That's bull." Says Ray. "In the last five years since I've known you, you've dated a string of women. Now you're in love with two of them again at the same time."

"Ray, it happens all the time. I don't like loving two women at the same time."

"I admire you as a bush pilot, your search and rescue folks in danger. But, this weakness when it comes to women. How long has this been going on?" Ray asks.

"I've had the desire since high school. I'm always in love with two women at the same time."

"You need help like from a love counselor or a psychologist."

"I can't get either one of the chicks off my mind. All day long, I think of them. I'd hate to lose either one of them," Frank says.

"Like all the rest of your women, that's what's going to happen."

"Do you really think I need to see a counselor?"

"That's your decision," Ray says.

* * *

Late at night, Frank tosses and turns in his bed and cannot sleep. He snaps on the television set, flips on various channels, and settles on Dr. Hung Low, known as the *Love Doctor.* "Doctor Hung Low speaking. Love is learned—everyone can and should learn to love. Vulnerability is always at the heart of love. But our vulnerability is the only thing we can give to other people. You must understand that if your love rejects you after a time, others wait for love. To think that there is but one right love is false. There are numerous right loves. You just have to use the correct techniques."

Frank sits up in bed and listens attentively as Doctor Hung Low continues, "To live in love is life's greatest challenge. In love, each of us face a personal challenge. We have no choice but to love."

Frank, wide eyed, moves closer to the television set and listens to Doctor Hung Low. "When we do not find where our alternatives lie," says Doctor Hung Low, "we'll have loneliness, destruction and despair. If you want to be a fabulous lover, you must start by saying yes to love and learn the right techniques to find your one-and-only. That's where I, Dr. Hung Low, comes in at my guidance center."

Frank snaps off the television set. Drowsy, he nods and mumbles, "I want to change my life, and I'll have to see Doctor Hung Low."

* * *

The next day Frank enters the revolving door of the Guidance Center in the glass and steel building complex on West Tudor Road. In one large gym, groups workout on treadmills, elliptical, exercise bikes, and power racks. On the left of the gym, people run on an indoor track. Down the hall from the fitness center, a sign hangs on a door:

Love Doctor. In the doctor's office, sits a receptionist. Beyond, a door leads to the doctor's private office.

Frank walks up to the receptionist.

"I'd like to see Doctor Low."

"Here, please fill in this form."

Frank takes the form, goes to a table, and completes the form. He returns to the receptionist's desk and hands her the form.

"Before seeing the doctor, you must prepare yourself by undergoing the conditioning requirements. Please enter the locker room, change your clothing, and put on the shorts and t-shirt an attendant will give you."

Attendants in separate rooms: weight, machine, steam, massage girls apply their disciplines. A technician in each discipline works intensely over Frank, pulling, slapping and jerking Frank's body. Frank works out on six weight-reducing machines. He huffs and puffs in another room with muscle building machines. Frank and another person drink water, and steam rises like a grey fog in the sauna room. Frank lies on a table. A masseuse loosens Frank's muscles.

When Frank completes his exercise and massage, he returns to Doctor Low's office.

"You may now see Doctor Hung Low," the receptionist says.

Frank enters Doctor Low's office. The doctor, dressed in a white medical smock, sits at a huge desk. He peers out of black-rimmed, thick glasses. Impressive diplomas hang on the walls.

"Hello doctor. You've been highly recommended. I find your name unusual."

The doctor laughs. "Yes, my name fits in how I help people. The patient comes in hanging low, and I pull them up hanging high." Doctor Low shakes Frank's hand vigorously and slaps Frank on his shoulder. Frank hands his medical questionnaire to the doctor.

"How do you feel?" asks the doctor.

"I feel crushed flat like a pancake. Those massage girls pounded on me like a punching bag. As a bush pilot, I get that same feeling when high winds toss my plane around. Why the rough treatment?"

"From the work over, you should feel physically rejuvenated. You will be in complete homeostasis. To eliminate your stress because of your condition. What's your problem?"

"Gosh Doctor Low, I'm always in love with two women at the same time. The problem is I Love both at first sight."

"Ah, yes. Sight love, a condition that saves a lot of time and money. Love is the only game that two can play and both win. How long has this been going on?"

"Since my senior year in high school, I've had trouble with my love life. I always am infatuated with two women at the same time. I want only one woman to love me, a woman to whom I could return love. I desperately need your help."

"Yes, yes this is very common. I've treated many patients with that problem with great success. Your two current women, tell me about them," the doctor says.

"I've tried to shake off this spell these two women have cast over me. In this situation, I see their beautiful faces in my dreams. I don't have the willpower to keep away from them."

"I think with my guidance and your help we can solve your problem. Your timing is excellent. Love is like the measles, all the worse when it comes late in life," Doctor Low says,

"I can't fight nature. I try to run from this terrible weakness. I'm like a hungry dog waiting for a bone. Do you think you could help me?"

The Doctor pounds desk. "Yes, I can throw you a bone."

"How long will it take?"

"That depends on you and the two women's suitability as to which one will make the best wife."

"Do I lie on a couch? I'm ready."

The Doctor blinks and rapidly explains. "When I want to use the psychoanalysis method, I use the couch. Primitive desires and instinct dominate the consciousness. This domination creates conflicts when inhibiting or controlling forces oppose the desires. For the most part, physiological needs are obvious. They are the literal requirements for human survival. These needs are those, such as breathing, food, water, sleep and elimination. If these needs aren't met, the human body simply cannot continue to function."

"I understand."

"That's good. Further up on the so-called Maslow Pyramid is love that includes friendship, family, sexual intimacy. This is where lots of people get into trouble because many of the drives are locked up in the sub-conscious. This is where my clinic can help with problems. Clear?

"Well, sort of. Doctor. Does my problem lie in my sub-conscious?"

"Of course, because they're in the unconscious part of your brain. We're not going to concentrate primarily on the subconscious, but we'll address behaviorist concerns that will improve your subconscious to some extent."

"Is that why I can't make up my mind about my women?"

The doctor blinks. "Exactly. The urges of the unconscious assume the task of compelling to repress unacceptable tendencies. Do I make myself clear?"

"I'm beginning to understand." Frank smiles.

"Now, you're going to combine the tests with behavioral tests that measure observable behaviors produced by a person's response to stimuli. The person uses low level processing skills."

"You mean like a woman brushing her hair or brushing her teeth?" Frank frowns.

The doctor pounds his desk. "Precisely. You've hit the nail on the head and the woman in her mouth."

"But, how do I decide which one is the best woman to love and marry? I love them both equally for different reasons. I thought I could be happy with one, and then I met the other."

"You're going to use some tests I'll give you in varying situations on each woman."

"I don't understand, doctor."

"The results of these tests will help you select the right woman for you. These are suitability tests. I'm not addressing your attraction to two women at the same time. Love is like a cigar, the brighter it burns, the quicker it turns to ashes."

"I'm ready to start your therapy." Frank breathes heavily.

"Remember, human beings tend to hide their big flaws. Little things reveal a person's character. Love may be blind but, you can't cover all the little imperfections."

"You mean like a woman wearing too much expensive jewelry or clothes?"

The doctor bangs his desk "You're right. Check each woman's jewelry box and each woman's walk-in closet for expensive clothing, and excessive jewelry."

Frank says, "That should be easy."

"Check each woman's hairbrush to see if she has removed excess hair. Check each woman's toothpaste tubes to see if they roll up the tube from the bottom. Then check the overall sanitation in the kitchens."

"What should I look for in the kitchen?"

"Well, like greasy spoons."

"That will be easy." Frank sighs.

"Check each woman's spending habits, their cooking, and their kindness to others."

"Doctor, how can I make sure I apply the same tests to both women?"

The doctor slaps Frank's shoulder. "That's real easy. Here's a list of tests you should follow. Each test on the list comes with short instructions to make the tests as scientific as possible."

"Thank you doctor. You've given me hope in my screwed-up life." Frank leaves the center and walks to his pickup. He muses, *I can hardly wait to find out if the tests are as reliable as Doctor Low says because I can't wait much longer for my lifelong mate. Doctor Low will not admit that any test he has worked out is a flub. Also, I have to have a series of reliable tests to select the woman of my dreams with whom I will live with and love for the rest of my life. I'm too old now to waste time frittering away my time with a series of women I am infatuated with. I have to shift gears from infatuation to true love.*

10

Lost Virginity

When Julie and Amanda bought the duplex, they agreed to exchange extra keys to use in case of emergencies. Julie returns to her apartment from her flight. With her emergency key, she enters Amanda's apartment.

"How's it going with Gus?"

"You know, as a supervisor on the Alaska pipeline," Amanda says. "He controls his subordinates by losing his temper and shouting at them. He does the same with me. With me, he is jealous and too possessive. His temper bugs me."

"Why do you stick with him?"

"Because, he's sweet to me and wants to marry me. His good looks—blond hair, big brown eyes—attracts me. At times, I think I could love him. Guess time will tell."

"Gus could change with your help. He could change his ways," Julie says.

"Maybe you're right—you've always given me good advice. Most of the time, Gus is fun to be with. But, when he loses his rotten temper, I don't like him. Really, he's too controlling."

Julie says, "I think he's worth a try."

Amanda replies, "Wish I could change him. I told him my feelings about his shitty temper, maybe he'll change."

As Amanda enters the bathroom, her phone rings.

"Answer the phone she shouts to Julie."

Julie picks up her message recorder and listens.

"Amanda I just want to say I miss you so much. Let's see each other soon. You stole my heart." Julie slams the phone down "Well, dear sister, so that's it! You seduced Frank."

"Who gave you the right to stick your nose into my business?"

"This is my business too. Frank is two-timing both of us. You enticed him."

"Listen, Julie, we can work this out."

"Work this out! Up to your old tricks again, this is the first time we've fallen for the same guy. I'm going to change that."

"It just happened. I can't back off," Amanda whines.

"How long has this been going on?"

"Only since you were on your flight to Tokyo. I didn't plan it that way. He already had bought the dance tickets for you and him."

"You didn't have to accept his invitation well knowing he bought the tickets for him and me, not you and him. You know I care about him."

"I couldn't help it. One thing led to another. It just happened that way."

Julie says, "So, you went to bed with him."

"That would be telling."

Julie says, "Well, I'm telling you, I went to bed with him. We made passionate love. Now he's mine not yours."

"Wrong, better we talk to Frank," Amanda says. "He wants me, whether you like it or not."

"You're lying. He needs me." Julie raises her voice.

"I don't have to put up with your lying crap. You've always been jealous of me, even in high school I didn't whore around, like you."

"Okay Julie! You should talk. You lost your virginity when you were a senior in high school. Don't call me a whore. You were the slut."

"I was what?" Julie shouts.

Amanda yells, "All the guys knew it." That's why you were so popular.

Julie's face contorts "You lying bitch, I'm tired of your bullshit."

Amanda smirks, "The truth hurts, doesn't it?"

Julie and Amanda scream as they shove each other around the room. Julie pulls Amanda's hair. Amanda punches Julie's nose which causes a nose bleed. They crash on the coffee table and wrestle on the floor. Amanda tears Julie's bloody blouse.

Amanda shrieks, "Get your fat ass out of here now, and give me my key back. Don't ever come back to my place again."

Julie throws the key at Amanda, and screams, "Leave Frank alone or I'll beat the hell out of you."

Amanda shoves Julie out of the door.

Julie returns to her apartment. "*Gosh, luck isn't on my side today. As Amanda asked me to do, I answered the phone. That's why Frank mistook me for Amanda. Oh well, I can't change that now. I'll have to be much more careful in the future. Otherwise, all will be screwed up with my relation with Frank. Frank is my type of guy and maybe he is Amanda's type too. I'll watch my step with the hope that all will turn out in my favor.*

* * *

Julie turns in her bed. In half-dreamland, she sees Frank who waits for her phone call. The morning sun shines bright through the window. She awakes with a start. "Gee, I am really in love with Frank. I can't get him off my mind.

Julie reaches for her cell phone and rings Frank.

"Hi Frank darling, I've got another long fight to Tokyo. I'll be back in five days. I miss you very much. We've got a lot to talk about. Do you still care about me?"

"I think of you every day. When you return, we can have some fun."

"I'd love that. Will you keep me warm?"

"You'll believe you're in the tropics. I have a special stove just for you."

"I have to run to catch my flight. I'll be thinking of you."

11

Cuddle up a Little Closer

Frank cannot control his compulsion. He telephones Amanda. "I can't forget the Jacuzzi. I miss you already."

"I miss you too. Come over now. We need to talk."

"I'll see you tonight about seven."

* * *

At seven sharp, Frank enters Amanda's apartment. She kisses him passionately and says, "You are always on my mind. I've never met anyone like you."

"I feel the same way about you. Julie's personality is so different from yours."

"Yes! You've got that right. We're so different in many ways. Absolutely!" Amanda says.

"Are you in competition with her over me?"

"For sure," Frank says, "I'm so sorry this has happened."

"I don't want to talk about Julie. Enough about me. Tell me more about yourself. I'd love to hear about some of your rescues."

"That would take all night. The wildest happened when I rescued a kidnapped banker ending in a shootout. I put a bullet between the killer's eyes. I'll tell you more later."

"Wow! I'll change the subject. Have you ever married?"

"I've never hung my toothbrush in a woman's bathroom."

"There're lots of eligible women in Anchorage. Why didn't the love bug bite?"

"Some did, but they didn't like the taste of me."

"Are you telling me you never fell in love?"

"No, I fell in love various times in my life. Lately, I never have the time to date much. I'm always on rescue missions."

"Are you going to make time now?"

"Yes, since I met you. And you?" Frank asks.

"I almost got married twice, but I couldn't tie the knot."

"I guess the unlucky guys regretted they missed the boat. Do you have anybody now?"

"I date a guy who wants to marry me, but I have doubts about him. Time will tell." "Do you ever want to get serious about marriage?"

"Sure, with the right guy."

Amanda pours a drink and Frank pulls her close on the couch. "You know, Amanda, I can't keep away from you."

"I hope it's more than just appearance. As a librarian, I know a person can never tell a story by the book title."

Frank stares into her eyes, "I want your story and the book to be a part in my life."

Amanda says, "Let's continue with the first chapter."

"Will you be ready for the last chapter?" Frank asks.

"What does that mean?" Amanda asks.

"Time does not wait, but fleets through events and vanishes."

Amanda winks, "I'll look into my crystal ball."

Frank holds Amanda close. She snuggles up and sings, "*Cuddle up a Little Closer*".

He kisses her with ardor and says, "Holding you close does things to my heart."

Amanda pleads, "Don't get a heart attack."

"If I did, I would be in your arms—then you could kiss me back to life." Frank whispers, "I can't believe this is happening. Your kisses mean something to me."

"I've kissed other guys, but their kisses left me cold as an ice cube. With you, I don't want it to stop. It's like a gift, but scary that it'll go away all of a sudden. I want us to get swept away and never lose our feelings." Amanda nods, "In a love story I read, the romantic people felt that a person would never know true love until they both give in to each other."

"That's very true. The world does go around on love. Love is what makes life worthwhile. Why don't we surrender to love now?" Frank asks.

Amanda says, "Because love takes time to develop."

"That reminds me of a poem I learned in a poetry class, '*To His Coy Mistress.*' by Andrew Marvell."

"Frank, do you want me to be your coy mistress?"

"Sounds like a great idea," Frank chuckles. "But you don't have to be coy. This is the end of the rather long poem." He recites.

> Let us roll all our strength and all
> Our sweetness up into one ball,
> And tear our pleasures with rough strife
> Through the iron gates of life:
> Thus, though we cannot make our sun
> Stand still, yet we will make him run.

Amanda laughs. "I'd rather eat some spinach for strength and sweetness."

"I feel like you put me on a starvation diet," Frank says. "Right now, I have to go on a rescue mission, which could be a long one. I'll be thinking of you."

Amanda's eyes light up. "Frank darling, I'll miss you very much. Please be careful, and I won't starve you when you return." She throws her arms around Frank and plants a passionate kiss on his semi-open lips.

"Wow, where did you learn to kiss the same way as the French do?"

"Kissing comes natural for me with the right guy. The guy has to be like you with lots of charm and love."

* * *

Five days later, Frank returns to his apartment from a rescue mission, exhausted and in muddy clothes. In a pent-up anticipation, he calls Julie.

"Julie. You are always in my thoughts. I've never felt this way before. I need to see you now."

"That makes two of us. I just can't stop thinking of you. My dreams about us are so beautiful."

Frank says, "I can't wait to hold you in my arms."

"Oh Frank, I'm sorry I missed you for our dinner date, but that's the nature of my job."

"Julie, I understand. Can you come over now to my place? We can make up for lost time."

"I'll be right over."

* * *

Julie arrives at Frank's apartment. She kisses Frank with pent-up passion. Frank slips his hand to Julie's blouse with the intent to unbutton it and move his hand to her breasts. Julie pulls away.

"Not now. I want to talk about us."

"At a time like this? You sure know how to make an excuse at the wrong time. Cold shower here I come."

"Not a too cold shower. Frank before we plunge into love making, we need to get to know each other better."

Frank asks, "Do you believe in love at first sight?"

Julie says, "Until I met you, it's never happened to me."

"It happened to me at our first accidental meeting on the ski slopes. Does your wristwatch keep the right time? I want to know how long it took before I went crazy over you."

"I'd be crazy if I didn't ask you if you are married. Do you have children?"

"I've never been married. No children I know of."

"How did you get around that?"

"I'm always rescuing lost folks in the wild. In my current job, I've never had much time for women. Again, I have to leave at 5 A.M. tomorrow on a search for two lost hikers."

"Now you want to make time for a woman?"

"Yes, time for you."

"I'm very much attracted to you. I'm willing to get to know you better. I'll take a vacation from my job."

Frank says, "I'll look forward to that. We can do many things in this great country of Alaska. It's the last frontier, and Anchorage is just as modern as the lower 48 State cities. I'll show you some unbelievable sights."

"Speaking of my 5 A.M. search mission, it's time for me to hit the pillow. Kick me out now."

"Under protest, I agree. I'll call you."

At the door, Frank and Julie hug and kiss with great passion.

"I missed you when you were flying."

"When I wasn't serving some unruly passengers, my thoughts went straight to you. I could hardly wait until my return to resume our loving dates."

Frank hugs Julie, kisses her passionately and exits the apartment.

Julie goes to the kitchen and makes herself a cup of steaming coffee.

On the sofa, Julie muses. *Frank's a nice guy; I have left the realm of infatuation with him to the area of real love. If he has the same feeling about me, maybe we can have a lasting relationship if he survives his dangerous career in the wild of the mountains in Alaska where animals could kill him, avalanches bury him or he could fall into a crevasse. It's a matter of luck. Luck was not on my side when I answered the phone and Frank thought he was talking to Amanda. I hope that blunder does not kill my chances with him.*

12

Puppy Love

On his return to Anchorage from his rescue mission, Frank visits Doctor Hung Low.

"How did the tests go?" the doctor asks.

"Only one woman passed the tests about cleanness and sanitation," Frank replies.

"Excellent, just excellent."

"I'm ready for the next set of tests."

"Find out whether the women are open to new experiences."

"Like what?"

Doctor Low scratches his head. "A tendency to be imaginative, independent, and interested in variety versus practical, conforming, and interested in routine."

"How do I do that?"

"Take them on a camping trip. Teach them how to fish, and skin a rabbit. You'll get a carload of information."

Frank says, "I'm concerned about money and their spending habits."

"Take them on shopping trips. Test to see if money is a primary goal in their lives. Or, is it a secondary in one or the other?"

"I've already checked their closets for expensive dresses, and jewelry boxes. What if they are neurotic?"

"Check to see if each woman is calm, secure, self-satisfied or anxious, insecure, and self-pitying."

Frank asks, "How do I find out if they are loyal, fun loving, sociable?"

"Take them to wild parties. Have a trusted friend hit on each one at the party to see if they are true to you."

"How do I find out if they are softhearted, trusting, helpful or ruthless, suspicious, uncooperative?"

"Find a drunk in an alley. See if she will take his wine away or take him home."

Frank says, "That could work to see if she has the heart to do that."

"I'm sure you noticed the dog kennel next to our clinic. We raise Siberian puppies to help in our therapies."

Frank, with a puzzled look, asks, "How can a puppy help my situation with the two women whom I love equally?"

The doctor smiles, "There's something irresistible about a Husky puppy in many ways. Their intelligence makes them special. That's why so many people have Huskies as pets."

"What's a puppy got to do with human behavior?"

"The puppy will react to emotional displays much like a person. We want both women to experience mothering the dog as a test to determine how suitable they would be in raising their own children."

Frank says, "I guess that makes sense. There're some women so attached to their dogs that they refer to them as 'my baby'."

"We rent the puppy to you complete with puppy food and instructions as to care for it. We provide vitamins with the puppy food."

"I understand. Doctor, your ideas are so different from what I know."

"I'm glad you recognize them. It will take some time for the suggestions to bear fruit. Here're the instructions. See me when you feel ready. You should take the puppy with you now."

Frank rents the puppy, attaches it to a leash, and takes the puppy to his apartment.

* * *

Ray enters and looks quizzically at the puppy. Frank holds the puppy in his arms.

"Do we now have to live with a dog?"

"This is only for a short time."

"Sounds like the doctor would do better with a skunk."

"So far, the doctor's advice makes sense. The doctor said the puppy helps me choose between the two women because it can show which girl has maternal instincts. The one who would make a good mother."

"I think you'll end up howling the dog blues. You'll lose both of the women," Ray says.

"Can I ask you to take the dog to Amanda? Tell her that I'm keeping the puppy for a friend, but that I have to go on a rescue mission. Tell her that you are unable to tend to the dog because you have work in Fairbanks."

"As a favor for you Frank, I'll go along with this doggie business. But, you may create two unhappy women, and you'll be like the song, 'Hound Dog', as Elvis Presley sang it:

> "You ain't nothin' but a hound dog
> Cryin' all the time
> You ain't nothin' but a hound dog
> Cryin' all the time
> Well, you ain't never caught a rabbit
> And you ain't no friend of mine."

Frank muses, I ain't no hound dog, but, it's getting more difficult to choose between Julie and Amanda.

* * *

Ray takes the puppy to Amanda's apartment. He puts the puppy on the floor.

"Frank is out of town," Ray says. "He asked me to deliver this puppy to you. He's holding the dog for a friend. Meet Snookie."

"What an adorable baby," Amanda says.

Ray hands Snookie to Amanda who cuddles the puppy.

"Frank hopes that you could take care of Snookie for a couple of days."

"I don't know anything about caring for puppies. Besides, I'm on call at odd hours at the library."

"If you have to work at the library on call, Frank asks you to take Snookie to Julie while he's away. He will be gone for less than a week."

"I guess I have no choice. I hope I can handle this."

"In any case, the experience will prepare you for motherhood."

"Think so? You're assuming my baby will turn out to be a dog?"

"You could write a book entitled *It's a Dog's Life*. At least, you could name your baby Snookie."

* * *

Amanda takes care of the puppy for three days. Three days later, Amanda goes to Julie's apartment.

"Hi Amanda, what do you have on the leash?"

"I was taking care of this puppy for three days to help Frank out when the library people called me to replace urgently a friend who has to have her appendix taken out. Ray asked me to take the puppy to you to take care of for a few days until Frank returns from a rescue mission. Here're two boxes of food and vitamins with instructions on what to feed the puppy." Amanda puts Snookie in Julie's arms.

"Meet your Snookie. He needs a mother."

"What a cute puppy!" Julie strokes his fur.

"Snookie is all yours. So play mother to him. It might be safer than loving a man."

"This is all I need to complicate my life. I'm off for five days. Had plans for those days not with a dog. I've heard the old joke, I'll be a monkey's uncle, but I've never heard I'll be a dog's mother."

* * *

When Frank returns to Anchorage, he thanks Julie and Amanda for their care of Snookie and returns the dog to his apartment. The next day he invites Julie and Amanda for lunch. The three enter *Sea Food's* a trendy restaurant near the seafront.

The waiter hands menus to all.

Julie asks, "What's your special of the day? I hope it's not fish."

"No. Bean soup of the day comes with a garden salad."

"I can't resist," Frank replies, "I order one."

Amanda tells the waiter, "I order a steak with all the trimmings. Cook it medium rare. Add a large shrimp salad."

Julie says, "I see the special is not good enough for your highness."

"You can mind your own business. I know what's right for me."

"That's a joke. I've never known you to be right about anything."

Frank says, "Can't you girls ever agree on anything?"

Julie shrugs, "You can see that our opinions and tastes are quite different."

Frank asks, "There must be something you can agree on."

Amanda replies, "Maybe we could agree if things ever get settled between us three, but I don't count on it."

"Now ladies! Remember the old saw, you can never win an argument. To change the subject, I would like to thank again you both for taking care of Snookie."

"Amanda dumped the doggie on me. It whined all night and dirtied my carpet. I couldn't sleep. After three days, I called Amanda to pick him up."

Amanda says, "I grew attached to Snookie. I loved it when he licked my face. I didn't mind cleaning up when he makes a mess. I even sang him to sleep."

"Hey, listen ladies how would you two like to attend a wedding next week? My old college buddy is getting hitched, and I'm the best man? It will be a formal affair."

Amanda replies, "I'd love to go, but I don't have an acceptable formal dress for a wedding." Frank smiles, "Why don't we go dress shopping now?"

The sisters reply in unison, "Great idea, let's go."

As they walk out of the duplex, Frank reflects, *Wow, now the game is approaching its end. After the trip to the dress shop, I might just be able to decide which one, Julie or Amanda, will be my one and only.*

13

Keep Outta My Pants

Julie, Amanda, and Frank enter a trendy bridal and bridal attendants shop in Anchorage.

At the dress shop, Julie and Amanda look for formal dresses suitable for attending a wedding.

Amanda says, "Thank you, Frank for inviting us to your friend's wedding. It's been a long time since I've gone to a formal affair."

Frank replies, "You'll look fabulous in what you chose."

Julie says, "Amanda doesn't always look good in her usual choice of a dress."

Amanda grumbles, "You should talk. You should see some of her gunny-sack dresses."

Julie and Amanda approach the sales person.

Amanda says, "I would like to see your formal gowns in red, size 6 or 8 strapless."

"Yes, Madame. We have some lovely dresses. Please follow me."

The sales person picks several red sizes, and hands them to Amanda. "Just step in the fitting room."

Amanda steps out of the dressing booth; she wears a bright red gown. "Frank, what do you think?"

"You look fabulous."

The sales person says, "I think the dress looks stunning on you."

Amanda turns and walks up to the mirror.

Julie says, "Are you kidding? The gown is too low cut. Your cleavage will get you arrested for indecent exposure."

Julie pulls up the top of the gown, and Amanda pulls it down.

"Keep your hands off. You don't have the boobs to show anyhow. So who are you to judge?"

"Your butt is too big. The size is all wrong," Amanda says.

"Frank, what do you think?"

"I like your butt."

The sales person agrees. "Your derrière looks fine."

Amanda tries on a beautiful tailored black dress.

"I like these two. There's a three hundred dollar difference. Which looks best, the black or red one?" Amanda asks Frank,

"Both colors are great." He points to the red dress. "You've got great taste."

Amanda says, "I like these two. But, there's a three hundred dollar difference." She turns to Frank, "Which looks best, the black or red one?"

Frank points to the red dress.

"I'll buy the red, the less expensive one," Amanda says.

Amanda looks at Julie "I don't splurge like you do. I like good value."

"I like good quality too, and will pay for the best. My three formals are in the closet. They still look great."

Both girls think they have outsmarted the other one. But which one will Frank choose, Julie or Amanda leaves them in doubt.

* * *

The next day Frank calls Amanda. Julie is in Amanda's apartment. "That's probably Frank." Amanda lifts the phone receiver; Julie takes up the extension.

"Are both of you ready for a quick camping trip?"

Amanda asks Julie, "What do you think?"

"I'm ready."

"Yes, we'll go." "Pick you up at 7 A.M. tomorrow."

* * *

Early morning Frank, Julie and Amanda climb into Frank's Piper P A -18 aircraft cockpit. At ten thousand feet, Frank decides to subject the two women to a stress tolerance test by placing the plane in a spin and dive mode.

"You probably know the thrill of a rollercoaster at the fair. We can get that feeling in a spin. Hang on," Frank says."

"This reminds me of my airline experiences in rough weather. It's just too scary. Stop it! It makes me too nervous," Julie shouts.

Amanda says, "I've always wanted to learn to fly. I love the feeling of falling in a roller coaster. Frank, don't pull out yet."

Julie squirms in her seat. "Pull out now or I'm going to throw up."

Frank pulls the plane up, and later lands on the beach on the Kenai. He sets up a tent and shows his rifle to Julie and Amanda.

Frank asks, "Ever shot a rifle before?"

Julie replies, "I've shot one at the county fair. Nothing to it."

Amanda says, "If that's so, how come you never hit the bull's eye?"

Julie replies, "You couldn't even hit the stand."

Frank hands his rifle to Julie. "Now girls let's decide who's the better shot. Aim at those two cans I've set up on the riverbank." He passes the rifle to Julie.

Wham, Wham. Julie sends both cans flying.

Frank, surprised, says "Great shots." He resets the cans and hands the rifle to Amanda. Wham, Wham. She misses, and the recoil knocks her back on her butt; she lands on a rock.

"Ouch! It's my shoulder, my butt. It feels numb. I'm going to have bruises. I feel like a horse kicked me."

"Let me take a look." Frank opens Amanda's shirt and inspects her shoulder. "Yes, the skin is red. You're going to have a black and blue spot. I'm so sorry. You should've cinched up the stock closer to your shoulder. Now I'll look at your butt. Open your pants."

"Leave my butt alone. You don't need to open my pants. Keep outta my pants."

"I thought you said you had a numbed butt. What if your butt is bleeding from a cut on the rock? You could get buttitis."

"Buttitis or not, you are not going to look at my butt. Julie can apply first aid if necessary. So just look the other way Frank." Frank turns and Julie inspects Amanda's butt.

"No cut, just red."

"Shooting is not for me. My butt can't stand it." Armanda rubs her bruise.

Julie says, "You're always afraid to try something new."

Frank suggests, "Let's try fishing. Some of the world's best fishing is here in Alaska."

They bait their fishing hooks while Julie stands on a boulder and throws out her line. A large fish hooks on her line, and jerks her off her feet. She falls into the rapids, and screams for help. Frank sprints downstream, dives in, and pulls her out.

Julie moans and says; "Frank, you saved my life. I'm so grateful."

Frank says, "Lady Luck is with us. I'm so happy, Julie, that you both made it out, but fishing is a waste of my time. I'd rather learn to bake a wedding cake."

"I'm always afraid to try something new?" Julie says, "Fishing is fun if you don't fall in the water."

Amanda replies, "Everything is fun for you. You need professional help from a psychologist or a psychiatrist. If you weren't so dumb you wouldn't have stood on that rock."

Julie frowns, "Since when did you become a shrink?"

"You've needed one for many years. Gus told me you don't know how to get serious about anything."

"Now ladies, let's not get nasty before our dinner. But first, we've got to dry our clothes."

Frank builds a fire. Julie strips to her bra and panties. Frank removes his clothing down to his underwear. He hangs the garments on tree branches.

Amanda says, "This is the closest I've come to a nudist colony."

Julie replies, "In a nudist colony, you'd be afraid to show your body. I think it would be exciting. What do you think Frank?"

"Both of you have fabulous bodies so cut out your arguing."

Frank opens a can of tuna and takes hardtack from his backpack. For dessert, he serves prunes.

Frank, Julia and Amanda eat beside the flickering campfire.

Julie smiles, "It's so beautiful here sitting under the stars. I love it."

Amanda points to the blinking big dipper. "Nature is so wonderful."

The mournful cry of a wolf echoes throughout the mountains.

Amanda points to the forest, "If you don't mind being eaten by wolves."

Frank stares toward the trees, "Not to worry, unless they are starving or have rabies they won't attack."

"That's not very consoling." Amanda frowns.

Julie says, "You're always worried about something."

Amanda shakes her head. "It's better than being in a dream world, like you always are."

Frank says, "Wolves rarely attack people."

Amanda says, "Tell that to the wolves after they have eaten us. Look! Two eyes glare at us."

"I see them." Frank picks up his rifle and races toward the forest. "Git, git, git, out, out!

The wolf takes off. "He's probably gone for good." Frank breathes hard.

Amanda frowns, "I wouldn't bet my life on it."

"I don't see how anybody can enjoy camping with those killers around. Camping is not for me. I'll take the parks and lakes in the city any time," Julie wipes sweat from her brow.

"Listen to the worrywart. I like camping and the outdoors. As long as I can shoot a rifle, I'm not worried," Amanda says, "You've only two shots one time today, and that was luck you hit the cans. You should be worried."

Frank points to the tent, "Time to sleep." He places his sleeping bag between Julie and Amanda who have separate sleeping bags. Julie says, "All our sleeping bags are open at the sides. That way we can all keep warm." Julie and Amanda snuggle close to Frank.

Julie asks Frank, "How do you like your harem?"

Frank smiles. "*When we three make love together.* Could we call it a *ménage à trois?*"

Julie says, "You might get a heart attack."

Amanda laughs. "Well, you'd die with a grin on your face."

During the night, Amanda slaps Julie, "Stop pushing me away from Frank."

"You stop doing the same to me."

Julie pulls Amanda's sleeping bag away from Frank. Amanda jumps out of her sleeping bag, and throws a punch at Julie who stands and counter punches wildly both screaming, and cursing. Frank separates them.

Frank mutters, "Children stop fighting over my body."

Julie touches Frank's arm. "I'm only protecting your tender body."

Amanda says, "Julie is so selfish. I'm the one that can save your body alone."

"I'm a homebody, not like you Julie. You're always travelling and out for excitement. My excitement is caring for the home."

Julie looks at Frank. "I want that too, and more."

Amanda frowns, "You're never satisfied with what you have. It's always fun and games with you."

Julie replies, "You're always looking for security. Everything is serious with you. You worry about everything. What a boring life."

Frank shakes his head. "Let's all get some sleep."

* * *

During the night, each sister continues to push away her respective bags close to Frank.

Julie pulls Amanda out of her sleeping bag. The tussle ends in a fistfight and hair attacks. Both sister's screams.

Frank separates the two. "Now children I will take away your lollypops if you continue to fight. Now I'm placed your bags way from each other so we all can sleep."

* * *

Early dawn, rain spills down with refreshing coolness. The rain stops. Frank, Julie, and Amanda break camp. The three of them plod along the scant trail. Julie ponders, *Frank will have to choose which one of us he wants. As it now stands, I don't know whether Amanda or I have Frank's heart.*

Frank's cell phone buzzes. "This is Ray. You just got a call from the airport rental at Merrill Field. One of their planes is missing. The pilot's flight plan indicates he was headed for the Kenai along the beach."

"I'll take off when the sun is higher in the sky."

Frank turns to Julie and Amanda. "Girls let's start breaking camp. We are going on a rescue mission."

When the sun is high in the sky and gives beter lightning for Frank to see a wrecked aircraft, he flies along the coast on the Kenai.

Frank points, "There it is! The wreckage on the beach."

Julie says, "It looks really smashed. I wonder if the pilot is alive."

"It looks like it flipped over. The cockpit is all bent out of shape."

Frank lands on the beach. The three rush to the wreckage.

Frank carries a first aid kit and enters the crushed cockpit. The pilot hangs upside down, held by his seat belt. Frank checks the injured pilot's pulse.

"The pilot is alive. He's still breathing. From the bump on his head, I think he may have a concussion. He could have had engine problems, tried an emergency landing, and the wheels stuck in the sand."

Amanda asks, "Why is the cabin so damaged?"

"Landing at high speed in fog could do it. I need both your help in trying to get him out. I'll bend back the door, try to push up the frame, and push him up while you girls un-snap his seat belt."

With great exertion, the girls unsnap the pilot's seat belt.

Together they place the pilot on the beach.

Frank calls the tower at Merrill Field.

"We found the crashed aircraft on the beach on the Kenai. The pilot is alive, looks like he had a concussion. I'll give him first-aid and fly him in. Please alert the paramedics."

Julie says, "He's still breathing with difficulty. Maybe he's got internal problems. I'll clean the blood off his head and patch up his cut with a bandage."

Amanda turns her head. "The poor guy. I just can't look anymore at his young face. It's making me sick."

"If you think this is bad, see what a grizzly can do to a face," Frank says.

Amanda frowns, "I just can't stand anyone who suffers. It's too depressing. I know your job is exciting, but it can be very sad. How do you keep from getting depressed?"

Frank says, "At times, depression grabs me. It's part of my job. Now we'll fly back to Merrill Field where the medics will be waiting."

Amanda asks, "Do you think he'll make it?"

Frank says, "Depends on the extent of his head injury. From my experience, I'd say he has a good chance of recovery."

Frank lands his plane at Merrill Field and turns the injured pilot over to the medics in the waiting ambulance.

* * *

Two Nights later, Frank, Julie, and Amanda go to a ski club dance. Frank guides them to Ray's table where Ray greets them. Ray says, "Nice to see you again."

Julie smiles, "My pleasure."

The band plays the bewitching song, *String of Pearls*. Frank escorts Julie to the dance floor.

Ray says, "I'm glad to see you again Amanda. May I have this dance?"

"I'm ready," Amanda grins.

They whirl around the room under the watchful eyes of Frank.

Amanda looks to the dance couples for Frank's approval. Frank glances over and nods.

"Amanda I would like to get to know you better. We had so much fun last time at Alyeska. Let's go for dinner? I promise not to bore you with engineering talk."

"Thanks Ray. I've got some decisions to make first. Maybe later. Thank you for the dance."

Ray smiles, "Dancing with you is like dancing with Ginger Rogers. So much fun."

Frank returns Julie to the table. Ray asks, "May I have this dance?"

Julie glances at Frank for approval. Frank nods he head.

On the dance floor Ray whispers, "Frank knows how to pick beautiful women."

Julie smiles, "Are you sure you're not mistaken? Beauty is in the eyes of the beholder?"

Ray laughs, "My eyes are not that old to judge beautiful women."

Julie says, "Beauty is only on the surface. Your mother should have taught you that."

"On behalf of my mother, could we get to know each other? How about it if I take you out to dinner?" "I would never want to hurt Frank. Thanks' for your offer and the dance."

Ray, disappointed, says, "I'm going to the bar and fill our glasses with the good stuff."

Ray ambles to the bar and fills the glasses. He returns to the table with four drinks. He reaches the table bends over and spills one of the drinks over Amanda's dress.

"I'm so sorry Amanda. Please forgive me. I'll pay for the cleaning."

"This is my most favorite dress."

"Let me send it to the cleaners."

"If the stain doesn't come out, what then?"

"I'll buy you a new one."

Julie says, "A good cleaning will take the stain out. The dress should be good as new. Spilling can happen to anyone."

"That's easy for you to say Julie. You're always broke because you're always buying new clothes."

"Give Ray some slack. He offered to pay for a new dress."

"I hope I don't need a new one," Amanda says.

"Again I'm so sorry. Please forgive me. It was stupid of me to carry four drinks."

* * *

A day later Amanda and Julie sit at Amanda's breakfast table.

Julie asks, "What do you think of Ray?"

"He's a good-looking guy with a personality—engineer type. He and I went to Alyeska."

"Why don't you go for him?" Julie frowns.

"You'd like that, wouldn't you?"

Julie says, "Maybe you're losing interest in Frank?"

Amanda shakes her head. "Ray asked me to dinner. I turned him down. I'm not giving up on Frank. Frank and I love each other, and always will."

"Ray invited me to dinner too. He's such a nice guy. As to Frank, let's set a date like two weeks to give Frank time to decide which of us two he prefers."

"So we give Frank an ultimatum," Amanda says.

"This is driving me nuts."

Amanda frowns, "Risky. We may force him to decide too soon; he may drop both of us."

"Are you up to it?" Julie asks.

"Yes, if you are," Amanda says, "Then it's settled, two weeks."

"What if he says he needs more time? Like another week?" Julie asks.

Amanda suggests, "Give him thirteen days, my lucky number."

"The thirteenth will be lucky or unlucky for one of us or neither of us."

"Before we call Frank, maybe Ray can help Frank decide." Amanda replies.

"You mean find out just what Frank's looking for in a woman. Frank doesn't know. That's his problem. A call to Ray won't help." Julie says,

"Not fair to both of us."

"I agree. We're in a crazy dilemma. Do we have much choice?"

Julie says "Let's call Frank, it's our last resort."

Amanda nods, "We'll invite him to our very special party. Maybe the party will motivate him to decide which one of us two he wants." Julie invites Frank, Ray, and Gusto the party.

* * *

Three days later the guests arrive, Julie turns on dance music. Both women wear low-cut dresses.

The table contains a variety of foods and hard liquor.

Julie fills glasses with Bordeaux wine.

"I propose a toast! May we all have many more fun years in the future?"

All raise their glasses and drink. They dance, and cuddle. Frank goes over to Amanda and Gus on the dance floor. "May I dance with Amanda?"

"This is the last time," Gus scowls.

Frank holds Amanda close. "I thought you might need to come up for some air."

"Gus means well."

"Why don't you tell him about us and put him out of his misery?"

"In view of the facts, that's selfish of you."

"I'm just trying to make it easy on you."

"That's a joke. This whole mess makes me very angry and sad."

Frank asks, "Do you think you caused part of this predicament?"

"So you think it's all my fault?

"I didn't say that."

Frank returns Amanda to the table. He pours himself another drink, and he cuts in on Ray and Julie.

"You're dancing very sexy with Ray."

Julia asks, "Why would you care?"

Frank answers, "You know our love dilemma."

"This whole conundrum stinks. You're the most selfish man I've ever met."

"I don't have to take this from you or any other woman. Dance with Ray. He's hot for you."

Frank and Julie return to the table. Gus and Amanda snuggle during the dance. Frank cuts in on Gus. Amanda cries.

"Hey, you jerk, nobody makes my girl cry."

"None of your business. Keep out of this."

"I'm making it my business." Gus shoves Frank. A fistfight follows. Ray separates them. "You keep away from my woman," Gus orders. "Or, I'll use you to mop the floor."

"You name the time or place."

"If I find you messing with her again. Watch out."

Julie says, "Hey guys, the party is over. Thanks for coming."

Julie escorts the men to the door.

Frank says, "I'm sorry that Amanda ended in tears. I had lots of fun until that bum, Gus, spoiled it. Goodnight," Frank slams the door.

Gus scowls, "If it weren't for that derelict, the party would have been great."

Ray smiles, "Thank you, I still think the party was fun, up to a point."

After the guests have departed Julie says, "It looks like we blew it tonight. This could be the end for both of us."

"In a way, I'm glad if it's over. To hell with Frank. I'm worried about Gus's threat. If Gus agrees to temper therapy, I could change. At times, I think I love him if it weren't for Frank."

Julie shrugs, "With Frank, we want the last word. We'll give him notice."

"You mean force his decision?"

"Give him a few days."

"Yes! Thirteen days, could be our bad or good luck. Thirteen is my lucky number." Amanda says, "He may have already dropped us. We'll see if Frank ever calls again."

14

Dilemma Drives Us Wacky

The next night Julie is in Amanda's apartment. The phone rings.

Amanda picks up the phone, and Julie listens on the extension.

"I want to apologize to you and Julie again," Frank clears his throat.

"Julie is here with me in my apartment. She is listening on the extension."

"I just had too much to drink. But, that's no excuse. Will you both forgive me? I should've backed off on Gus." Frank coughs.

Julie and Amanda say in unison, "Can you come over now?"

"I'll be over right away."

Amanda says to Julie, "Then it's agreed. We stick to thirteen days for him to decide."

Frank arrives at Amanda's apartment. "Let's forget about last night. Do you still feel the same way about us?" Amanda asks.

"There's no change in my feelings for both of you."

Julie nods, "We're all on the same boat, but the Titanic is slowly sinking. You expect this to go on forever?"

"This is driving us wacky." Amanda shrugs.

"Whose fault is all of this? You're the one who couldn't make a decision when you began the relationships," Julie says. "Look Frank, Amanda and I have decided that if we all can't decide within thirteen days which one of us will be in your future, it's all over with us."

"So, you think threatening me is the answer. You're sandbagging me. Do you think it's easy for me? Loving both of you the way I do."

Amanda says, "We are giving you time to decide. If you haven't decided by thirteen days, then we'll decide—it's quits for both of us."

"I don't need thirteen days." Frank bangs his fist on the table and rushes out the door. Julie shakes her head.

* * *

In the evening, Ray calls Amanda.

"I'm so sorry about the party. I'll take you out to the ski club for dinner tomorrow evening at seven. Dinner at the ski club might cheer you up."

"I'm very upset the way things are turning out because of Frank. I need to talk to you. I'd love to go to dinner at the ski club."

Amanda calls Julie. "Ray asked me to dinner tomorrow evening. What do you think?"

"Okay. At least you can talk about it."

Ray and Amanda have dinner at the ski club. Frank enters the club and sits alone at a table at the end of the dance floor.

"Ray, you know our story. It's driving us crazy. You know Frank very well. What do you think? Is it hopeless? Frank is the first guy my sister, and I have fought over. We sisters used to be close, but not anymore."

"Frank is very vulnerable. He probably protects himself by having two women on the string at the same time. Give him a little time. I'll do what I can to help him make a decision. But he needs help from you and Julie."

"What kind of help?"

"You make him jealous."

"How do we do that?"

"I'll show you."

Ray and Amanda cuddle on the dance floor. Ray kisses Amanda and waves to Frank.

Frank leaves the ski club alone without acknowledging Ray and Amanda.

Ray struggles to get up from his chair to leave.

"It's my back pain; I can't seem to shake it. The doctor has tried everything."

"Tried massage? That's something I know about. Come with me."

"I'll try anything."

At Amanda's apartment, she says, "Take your shirt off. Drop your pants down to your shorts."

She deep rubs and kneads on Ray's spine.

"Hey! Your magical fingers hurt."

"It's really simple. Lack of oxygen to the tissues causes muscle pain. I'm bringing circulation to the muscle by rubbing."

"I feel better already."

"If I keep working at it, your muscle will rebound into a relaxation mode."

"Let's continue this relaxation mode for the future."

"I can't promise the future."

"Let me try to help," Ray pleads.

Back in Frank's apartment, Ray says, "Thanks for allowing me to meet your women. They're both terrific. I hope you are not pissed."

"Not at you. I gave both women tests and found they both scored differently, but overall, they scored equally. Now I'm back to where I started. I didn't like their thirteen-day ultimatum for me to decide, and I walked out. Anger got the best of me."

Ray says, "I have to tell you that I'm in love with Amanda."

"What! So, you are trying to cut me out."

"It just happened. I'm sorry to mess things up. Amanda has agreed to date me for the next month."

"This gives her time to decide on Gus, or me regarding future dating."

Frank says, "I've lost both women. I've hurt both sisters. It's been hell for us all. After meeting Julie, it was harder for me to admit I had fallen in love for Amanda. I blew it. After all, with Doctor Hung Low's tests I've learned that love has everything to do with my heart and not with cold reason."

* * *

One week later, Frank writes an invitation to Julie and Amanda to Ray's surprise birthday party.

Julie calls Amanda. "I'm surprised at his invitation."

"We should go and tell him we still love him."

"I agree. I'd like to see Frank's reaction when he sees us. Speaking of reactions, how is Gus faring with his temper management therapy?"

"Not working. On our last two dates, we had a terrible time. It's over with us."

"Sorry, Julie says, in a sad voice.

At Frank's party, all gather around the coffee table on which is a chocolate birthday cake, and four bottles of champagne. They sing happy birthday to Ray who blows out thirty candles. All raise their glasses to toast Ray. After the party Ray thanks every one, and departs to the airport, to fly to Fairbanks to inspect a building.

Frank says, "I want you to know there has been no change in my love for both of you." He embraces Julie and Amanda.

Julie says, "We want you to know that we continue to love you in our own ways."

Back in her apartment Amanda muses, *I think of others who depend on our decisions; there's Ray and Frank who* await Julie's and my decision. *It looks like Father Time will provide the answer. Will I find a guy with whom I can happily spend the rest of my life? Well, Frank really interests me with his talents, and he is attracted to me. I must watch myself because Julie also has the hots for Frank. Only time will tell.*

* * *

A month later Amanda talks to Julie. "In our situation where all of us are involved one of us has to break the stalemate. My mother taught me a bird in hand is worth two in the bush. Dating Ray has been wonderful. I know now I'm in love with him when he proposed marriage, and I said yes."

Julie replies, "I'm so grateful for your decision."

15

A Rain of Rose Petals

Three months later, Julie's and Amanda's prophesy becomes true. The sisters announce their double wedding.

Twenty-five invitees assemble at the Anchorage Lutheran Church. At the altar, two couples kneel and face Pastor Sverre Michalson. The two Maids of Honor and the two Best Men stand at the couples' sides.

Pastor Michalson proclaims. "We are gathered here today to witness the joining of two different couples in matrimony. This wedding is by far the most significant symbol of lifelong personal commitment between two individuals. In essence, being engaged, inviting your friends and family, scheduling a fancy party, and booking a honeymoon are indeed forms of commitment as well. However, ultimately, none of these financial obligations means anything until, like today, you stand in front of everyone, and recite the Christian wedding vows. A wedding is a pledge, a promise to devote yourself to each other till death do you part."

"Will the grooms please repeat after me? *I do solemnly declare that*

I know not of any lawful impediment why I, (each groom says his name), may not be joined in matrimony. Pastor Michalson looks at the brides, and repeats the question he asked of the grooms, the brides reply to Pastor Michalson's questions.

Pastor Michalson asks, "Is there anyone here today who knows any reason why the marriage couples should not be joined in matrimony?

No person replies.

Pastor Michalson proclaims, "I now pronounce Frank Carlton and Julie Kittleson together with Ray Walker and Amanda Ulland husbands and wives."

The two Best Men give the grooms the wedding rings. The two Grooms slip the rings on their respective Brides' ring fingers.

Frank and Julie at the same time with Ray and Amanda kiss and turn toward the aisle. The organist plays Johann Pachelbel's Cannon in D for the procession to stroll down the aisle.

The invitees raise a loud applause as Frank and Julie together with Ray and Amanda slowly march along the aisle under the sweet music from the organ. The two married couples step through the open church door. The attendees at the wedding shower the two couples in a rain of rose petals.

Frank and Julie together with Ray and Amanda and the attendees return to the church. They enter a joining room for the wedding party. Frank and Ray cut a huge wedding cake. The brides pass the pieces of cake to the guests.

Doctor Hung Low steps close to the Frank and Julie together with Ray and Amanda. He shakes the married couples' hands and says, "I am so happy for all four of you.

"Thank you so much" Frank and Julie together with Ray and Amanda reply in unison to Doctor Hung Low.

16

Ten Years Later

Frank, president of his privately owned company Search and Rescue Inc., stands with Julie and six company pilots in front of his company's headquarters building in Anchorage.

Ray, president of his privately owned company United Tourist Travel with offices throughout the world, and Amanda embrace each other in front of his company headquarters in Tokyo.

Nine years ago, Gus married his high school sweetheart. They pose for a selfie in front of his machine shop in Anchorage.

THE END

Printed in the United States
By Bookmasters